Albert
and the
Magician

Leon McAuley

Illustrated by Martin Fagan

THE O'BRIEN PRESS
DUBLIN

First published 1996 by The O'Brien Press Ltd,
20 Victoria Road, Dublin 6, Ireland.
Tel: +353 1 4923333; Fax: +353 1 4922777
E-mail: books@obrien.ie
Website: www.obrien.ie
Reprinted 1999.
This edition first published 2002.
Reprinted 2004.

ISBN 0-86278-761-0

British Library Cataloguing-in-Publication Data.
A catalogue reference for this title is available from the British Library.

Editing, typesetting, layout, design: The O'Brien Press Ltd
Printing: Cox & Wyman Ltd

For Alicia, Ben and Daniel

Contents

A Very Interesting Announcement

ALBERT'S BIG SISTER, Fionnuala, was an expert on magicians. Pudgy, smarty-pants Fionnuala was an expert on most things, except for moving about without falling. This was her one and only flaw. Fionnuala was thaveless. She was, without question, the world champion at cutting her knees, knocking things over and crying her eyes out – that's what thaveless means. But it was only a few days ago that Albert had discovered she was an expert on magicians. It was on Monday at Assembly.

Albert didn't like Assembly. Albert didn't like school. Next Friday, school was breaking up for the summer holidays. Albert was looking forward to next Friday with all his heart, all his being, all his might and all his teddy bears. They were packed in his sports bag with Tony, the Bengal tiger who slept with Albert, and a book about birds of prey. Albert was ready for the road.

In fact, Albert had thought about hardly anything except next Friday since last Friday. It must have been at least three days since he had even looked at his book about birds of prey, let alone drawn an eagle or thought about wildlife. Usually he was *always* thinking about wildlife. Wildlife was all the animals you didn't eat, plus cows. He had always loved cows. It was something to do with their big, black, watery eyes; their big, black, clear, watery nostrils; their big, rough, pink tongues and their warm, green, milky smell. Albert just loved cows. But all he could think about these days was the school holidays and freedom – weeks and weeks of freedom and adventure!

At Assembly on Monday morning the headmaster, Mr Curry, The Chicken, had made a very Important, Interesting and Exciting announcement. Albert was bored. The only thing that was important, interesting and exciting as far as he was concerned was that school was breaking up on Friday.

'Now, boys and ... *bwook* ... girls, I have a very Important ... *bwook* ... Interesting and Exciting announcement to make,' said The Chicken. Albert didn't like The Chicken. He especially didn't like the way you could see the hair in The Chicken's nostrils and ears. There was tonnes of it. It poked out of his nose, looking like dead whin bushes. It wafted in the breeze when you were getting a telling-off. When Mr Curry was really mad it kept disappearing and then shooting back out again as his breathing got louder. Albert's keen eye – one-hundred-and-two-and-

a-half centimetres from the ground – had often noticed this as he stood, three buttons up from the bottom of The Chicken's waistcoat, getting 'what for'.

'On Thursday,' Mr Curry continued, the hair in his nostrils wafting gently, 'because the ... *bwook* ... holidays are coming, we are having a ... *bwook* ... visitor. His name is The Great ... *bwook* ... Gazebo. I wonder if you can guess what he is? Put up your hand if you want to have a ... *bwook* ... a guess.'

The Chicken put his hands behind his back, stuck his waistcoat buttons out, waved his elbows in and out and rocked back and forth on the heels of his brown brogue shoes. He always wore brown brogues. They went with his three-piece suit. The waistcoat had seven buttons. Albert had counted them several times. And the suit was the colour of ... well, Albert didn't want to think what the suit was the colour of, but it was something connected with cows, and it was very hard to get off your shoes. That's exactly the colour The Chicken's suit was. That's why the brown brogues went with it. He had worn them for so long that the heels were completely worn down at the outsides. Albert knew this because he had followed Mr Curry to the office so often with his head down trying to think of a good excuse. And always, when you're trying to think of a good excuse, you notice the strangest things. It's as if your mind wants to run away.

'Anybody like to *hazard* a ... *bwook* ... a guess?' The Chicken said again, the hair in his nostrils shaking like a whin bush in a hurricane as he said the word 'hazard'. Obviously he thought this was an extremely amusing word. Albert didn't. He hadn't a clue what on earth the person who was coming could be, but he thought that anybody with a name like The Great Gazebo would have to be pretty spectacular to excite him. The Great Gazebo? It sounded like a cross between a fat gnu and a garden shed. A gnu – and Albert always pronounced the 'g' in gnu – was a big African antelope. Albert knew about gnus because gnus were wildlife.

'Who'd like to guess what The Great Gazebo might ... *bwook* ... be?' The Chicken asked again, still rocking on his heels.

Everybody round Albert put up their hands, so Albert put his hand up too. All the seniors from Primary Seven were sniffling and shuffling, whispering and snoggling, pretending that they all knew and were having to try very hard not to shout out the answer so that they wouldn't get into trouble. Albert still hadn't a clue, but he felt safe. The Chicken wouldn't ask *him*. The Chicken never did. He probably thought it was too dangerous. You never knew what strange and not necessarily wonderful thing Albert would come out with. The Chicken knew from experience that asking Albert was not a good move. Sometimes Albert got the feeling that The Chicken didn't like him very much. He asked Julie instead.

'Well, Julie?' asked The Chicken.

See! thought Albert. I knew he wouldn't ask me. But he took his hand down anyway, just in case. Albert had done his bit: he didn't want to push his luck. Albert knew from experience that luck was not something he had enough of to push.

'Please, sir,' said Julie, who probably went to elocution and ballet dancing, 'I think he might be a photographer.'

'No, Julie ... *bwook* ... but that was a very good guess,' said The Chicken. Then rocking crazily on the backs of his brogues he added, 'Wasn't it, boys and ... *bwook* ... girls?'

'Yes, sir,' said all the boys and girls together in a sing-song sort of voice.

'Peter?' asked The Chicken.

Albert froze. Peter was one of Albert's two closest friends. Indeed, at this very moment he was sitting right beside him. Being a close friend is one thing, but this was too close for comfort.

'Please, sir, is he the doctor or the dentist?' Peter asked, twirling the hair above his right ear round his pointing finger. It was something he always did when he was nervous. It always made Albert smile.

No way, Peetie baby, thought Albert. Miles out, boy. Albert always knew what things weren't, even if he didn't know what they were. He was right again.

'No, Peter, someone far more ex ... *bwook* ... exciting than that. But it was a good guess anyway,' said The Chicken.

Well, that doesn't say very much for The Great Gazebo, does it? thought Albert, who could hardly imagine anybody *less* exciting than the doctor or the dentist.

'Anybody else?' asked The Chicken.

It's only a matter of time, Albert thought.

Our Miss Smarty-Pants Fionnuala is bound to put her hand up.

'Feewonuuuuwalla?' said The Chicken – no, he didn't actually say it, he skied down it. Albert had been right again.

Here we go, thought Albert, and as Fionnuala spoke, he quietly hummed the tune: 'Here we go, here we go, here we go ...'

'Please, sir,' said Fionnuala, 'in one of my books – I think it might have been a book of fairy stories – there was a man called The Grand Vizier, and he was a kind of magician.'

'Here we go, here we go, here we go-ho ... get on with it, ugly ...'

'Good girl, Feewonuuuuwalla! That's exactly what The Great Gazebo is. He's a mag ... *bwook* ... magician, a real, live magician!' said The Chicken. 'Now, isn't that exciting?'

Of course! thought Albert, who had stopped humming now. He's a real, live magician! He wouldn't be a real, *dead* magician, would he?

He had just remembered about the Great somebody-or-other on television. He wished he'd remembered about him earlier, then maybe Fee-won-uuuu-walla wouldn't have been ahead of him. It wasn't that he was jealous of Fionnuala – well, perhaps a little bit – it was just that *he* was clever too, and that nobody ever paid him any attention!

Then Albert started to think about the magician. He didn't know if this was exciting news or not. He liked the magicians he had seen on TV, except when they used pigeons or rabbits, which were, of course, wildlife. Albert didn't like cruelty. He liked it best when they did that trick where they would saw a lady in half. Albert saw a lot of potential in that particular bit of magic and he knew *exactly* who he would pick as the lady. But Dad said that what those magicians did wasn't real magic, it was just camera trickery.

While Albert was thinking all this a shiver of

excited noise was going round the assembly hall.

'Isn't that exciting?' The Chicken asked again.

'Yes, sir!' all the pupils said together – all except Albert. After The Chicken's brief interruption Albert had returned to his murderous thoughts about Fionnuala. Now he was thinking: Isn't it just like that big horrible plip-plop of a sister of mine to get the answer right?

He looked over his shoulder. Just as he expected. There was Fionnuala sitting in the middle of all her rotten big friends with a really dozey smile on her face. When she saw him looking at her she put her head to one side and half-closed her eyes and gave him a sarcastic smile. He gave her a sarcastic smile back, putting his head to the other side. She made a face and stuck out her tongue at him, so what did Albert do? Albert did what anybody, especially an Albert, would have done under the circumstances – he made a face right back and stuck his tongue out at her too.

'Albert!' The Chicken guldered, turning the colour of beetroot, even the hairs in his ears blowing in *this* hurricane and the buttons of his waistcoat creaking under the strain. 'I saw that!'

Typical, thought Albert. Typical, typical, typical, typical …

'Turn around, please! All of you turn around!' The Chicken continued, his voice and his colour returning to normal. 'So, boys and girls, I want all of you to bring fifty … *bwook* … pence to school tomorrow and we'll see the magician on Thursday. I'm sure you will all be looking … *bwook* … forward to it. Now, everybody, off you go to class … except you, Albert! You wait for me at the door of my … *bwook* … office, please!'

Bwook, bwook, *bwook*, BWOOK! thought Albert. That was why he hadn't wanted to push his luck.

CHAPTER 2

Break, Break, Break!

'PUSH ON, MCKEOWN,' growled Albert.

It was break-time. He was flying in close formation with the two terrible Peters, P1 and P2 as he called them. Nyrrrrrr ... they were on a rescue mission. They were trying to rescue the brand new football that Steven Kennedy in Primary One had brought to school. When they had rescued it, they would play with it until the bell went. They might have to let Steven play too, but that was the price you had to pay.

Albert almost touched wings with P2 as they shot around the corner of the dining hall and flew slap bang into the Three Musketeerettes – Fionnuala, Anita and Siobhan. Vrrooommmm ... it was too late to eject ... Vrrooommmm ... Albert banked steeply to the left and dived. Nyrrrrrrn ... it didn't work. Usually he was far too quick and flexible for Fionnuala, but this time she caught him by the shoulder.

'Not so fast, Small!' she said. Albert hated it when she called him 'Small'. 'I hope you're not chasing the wee men in Primary One again?'

Albert pulled away.

'Leggoamee! Aaaahwasn't!' Albert shouted. He was getting mad. When Albert got mad he started to speak in a foreign language – a language closely related to English, but not quite English. He pulled his shoulder free. 'Luggaatt wattyavdun toomaJERSEY!'

Fionnuala knew, of course, that Albert would get mad. She was doing this on purpose. She didn't care *that* much about protecting the wee men in Primary One from low-flying

Alberts, though she could have convinced herself that she did. Right now Fionnuala wanted to Get At Albert, and far more than anything else that she was an expert at, far more than magicians or bursting into tears or even falling down, Fionnuala was an expert at Getting At Albert.

Fionnuala was, in fact, one of the sweetest and gentlest girls you could ever meet – she was intelligent, sensitive, imaginative, creative, concerned, patient, caring, funny, obedient and reliable. She was *almost* perfect. But being almost perfect is a Big Responsibility, and people can very easily get the wrong idea about you. Fionnuala did not want people to think she was a goodie-goodie. But if you are intelligent and reliable and always get most of your homework right and do what you have been told just the way whoever asked you wants it, people, especially teachers, pick on you all the time. They ask you to run messages and clean up and bring around the roll books and beat the duster and look after things in general, and before you know it everybody is saying: There goes Fionnuala, the goodie-goodie! It gets very frustrating, and when you get frustrated you take it out on somebody, and the somebody you take it out on is somebody that you love and that you know loves you back.

Albert and Fionnuala *had* to love each other – they were brother and sister, after all. If you asked Fionnuala did she love Albert she would say: Yes, I suppose I do, but that doesn't mean I have to *like* him, does it? Splitting hairs was one of Fionnuala's hobbies. She was very good at it.

But if you asked Albert the same thing about Fionnuala he would have told you straight out: She's a big fat plippy-plop and I can't stand the sight of her! That would be Albert's way of saying: Yes, of course I love her. What a stupid question!

'I thought you'd have had enough trouble today already,' said Fionnuala, with her pretty-little-pink-nose stuck up in the air.

Fionnuala was very fond and proud of her pretty-little-pink-nose. It was one of her favourite organs. She thought it looked really pretty and she used it as much as possible. The thing she did least with it was breathe through it. In fact, Fionnuala said more with her nose than she did with her mouth. She was a woman of few words, a speak-if-you're-spoken-to-but-only-if-you-really-must type of girl, but she could tell you exactly how she was feeling and what she thought just by the way she pointed her nose. She used it to emphasise things. She used it to show when she understood something, and when she didn't understand something; to show how much she liked things and to show how much she hated things.

At the moment the nose was somewhere up between her eyebrows, letting Albert know that she regarded him as slightly lower down the ladder of evolution than a ring-tailed lemur.

'Well, it was you who got me into it!' Albert snarled. He was beginning to calm down and speak English again.

Fionnuala could tell he was annoyed, so she suddenly became very concerned and sweet and gentle, and that, as she knew it would, got Albert really mad. She relaxed her nose and turned it down like the heat on a cooker. 'But I didn't mean to get you into trouble, Albert. Anyway, you were the one who was jealous, so you deserved it. The Chicken wasn't too cross with you, was he?' She was dying to hear all the gory details of what the headmaster had done to him.

Albert wasn't going to tell her though. 'Nunayerbusiness,' he growled and ... Nyrrrrrrn ... pulled away from her and flew off to join the supersonic Ps who were circling over the horizon, out of harm's way behind The Chicken's car, waiting to resume their mission to rescue wee Steven Kennedy's football from the evil clutches of ... well, of wee Steven Kennedy. *Nyrrrrrnnnnnnnnnn...* ...

CHAPTER 3

Home for Tea

WHEN THEY GOT HOME that evening Albert and Fionnuala told their mother all about the magician coming to school. Mum was a small, cuddly woman whom Albert liked very much, but she always had other things on her mind. She usually wore one of those plastic aprons that have jokes written on them. Tonight it said: JUST SIT QUIETLY AND SEE HOW THINGS PAN OUT. It was good advice at dinnertime in Albert's house.

'Gosh! I bet you're very excited, aren't you?' Mum said, though Albert got the feeling that she wasn't really listening very hard. She was lifting hanks of real spaghetti from a big saucepan into a colander with a red plastic back-scratcher, and shooing away clouds and clouds of steam with her other hand.

Eugh! thought Albert, spaghetti! Albert did not like spaghetti.

'How much does it cost to get in?' asked Mum.

There was a pause while Albert tried to figure out what she was talking about. Then he remembered – the magician. 'Fifty pence each,' said Albert.

Mum ignored him and said over his head, 'Fionnuala, I'll give you the one pound ...'

'Sorry?' said Albert, pulling himself up to his full hundred-and-two-point-five centimetres. 'Am I *invisible* or WHAT?'

'What?' asked Mum. 'Albert, don't interrupt!'

Fionnuala smirked and her pretty-little-pink-nose came as close as a human nose can come to doing a somersault.

'Fionnuala, I'll give you the one pound to pay for yourself and Albert. I can trust you to keep it safe and not to lose it, can't I?' Mum hauled another consignment of wriggly stuff out of the saucepan. 'Go and wash your hands, the pair of you, and I'll call you when dinner's ready – and don't waken The Twins!'

It just wasn't fair, Albert thought as he made for the stairs. Mum always gave Fionnuala money to take to school for both of them. Why didn't she trust him? After all, he was a big boy now. He was seven. He was in Primary Three.

Still, it was a good thing that Mum was so busy. There hadn't been time for Fionnuala to tell how Albert had got into trouble at Assembly that morning. He looked back through the open door into the kitchen. Mum was jul-*ienne*-ing carrots and de-*glacé*-ing pans and opening cans of tomatoes, all of which were bad signs for Albert. Albert hated fancy food. He was a beans-with-everything man. A

thought occurred to him and he sauntered back into the kitchen. 'Do you know what I think would be magic, Mum?' he asked. Mum was doing something fairly violent to a clove of garlic with what looked like a pair of pliers.

'What, Albert?' she grunted.

'I think it would be magic if you could turn all that horrible fresh good-for-you food into something really tasty like a plate of beans for me,' said Albert.

'Do you now, Albert?' Mum grunted again. She pulled herself up to her full five-feet-one-and-a-half inches – she was born before decimalisation. Actually, she claimed to be five-feet-one-and-three-quarter inches, but this did not matter to Albert, since he only understood centimetres. She pulled herself up to her full five-feet-one-and-a-half inches and came down heavily on the pliers. 'Go and wash your hands right this minute!' She was squeezing really hard on the pliers and she was thinking about Albert's ears. So Albert disappeared up the stairs.

While they were washing their hands in the bathroom, Albert said to Fionnuala: 'What does a real magician do, Fionnuala? Is he like the magicians on TV? Dad says they're not real magicians and that most of the things they do are just camera trickery. What does a *real* magician do?'

'You mean you don't know, Albert?' said Fionnuala, her pretty-little-pink-nose leaping into action. She was smirking again, and squeezing together the palms of her hands, making a grey gloop of soap suds rise like lava over her grubby thumbs.

Honestly! Big sisters can be really annoying sometimes, Albert thought. If he knew he wouldn't have asked, would he? And he squeezed his hands together too, but hard, so that his grey gloop of soap suds shot right into the air and landed in an exclamation-mark shaped blob on his school trousers.

Before he could ask again, Mum called the two of them down for dinner.

Fionnuala said: 'We'd better go down now or Mum will get mad. She'll be mad anyway when she sees that soap on your good school trousers. She'll kill you! Come on. I'll tell you all about magicians later,' and the two of them went downstairs to their diet of worms.

During dinner there was, as usual, a lot of talk about wee-starving-children-in-the-Third-World because Albert would not eat his dinner. Fionnuala was being particularly troublesome too, and Albert was dreading everything she said because he knew that sooner or later she would spill the beans on him about Assembly. So when Mum got very cross because Dad was working late and because of all the carry-on and decided to send the two of them straight to bed, Albert was relieved and quite pleased. He had just remembered that Fionnuala had promised to tell him all about real magicians.

CHAPTER 4

What is a Real Magician?

'WELL THEN, WHAT *IS* A REAL MAGICIAN, Fionnuala?' Albert asked when they were getting ready for bed.

'You mean you don't know?' said Fionnuala. She was picking her toenails with her finger and she didn't look up. 'Well ... there ... are ... lots ... of ... different ... kinds ... of ... magicians,' she said, picking away.

'But what do they look like?' asked Albert.

'Well ...' said Fionnuala, 'mostly they wear baggy trousers made of silk and they wear curly-toed satin slippers and waistcoats all embroidered with beautiful designs and no shirts ...'

'No shirts?' said Albert, and you could tell from the sound of his voice, which was very quiet and slow, that his eyebrows were beginning to rise and a white ring was starting to appear around his mouth. By now he was getting into bed.

'No shirts ... and they have big hairy chests and big muscles with copper bracelets and bangles at the tops of their arms. They wear hats that look like lampshades with flowerpots on top. They have dark, swarthy skin and thin black moustaches that curl up at the ends and they always wear one earring ...'

'One earring?' said Albert, whose eyebrows had by now gone so far up his forehead that they were almost behind his ears. That settled it. He knew for certain he'd never seen a real magician before. He should be able to spot The Great Gazebo without any difficulty at all.

'I do wish you wouldn't repeat every word I say,' said Fionnuala in her extremely-grown-up voice. Fionnuala's extremely-grown-up voice really annoyed Albert. It wasn't quite as annoying as her deeply-concerned-and-caring voice, but Albert knew she only used that when she had some real humdinger of a trick up her sleeve. And then it came.

'They're seven feet tall ...'

'What are?' asked Albert.

'Magicians!' said Fionnuala. 'Now, pay attention.'

'Right!' growled Albert.

'They're seven feet tall and they stand with their arms crossed and they laugh like this,' Fionnuala looked up for the first time from picking her toenails, took a deep breath, folded her arms and went, 'Eey-hay-hay-hay, eey-hoo-hoo-hoo, uhh-uhh-a-hey, he-hay, he-hoo.'

It was a tremendous performance, even for Fionnuala. The room seemed to shake and

Albert's blood ran cold. The hairs on the back of his neck stood up – both of them.

Then a voice from downstairs shouted, 'What was that? Are you two not asleep yet?'

'Nothing, Dad! Just getting into bed! Night-night!' shouted Fionnuala.

Albert's blood may have been running cold, but he still managed to think to himself that big sisters are really dopey. It was *genies* she was thinking about.

'That's genies!' said Albert. Albert knew all about genies.

'You mean, "those are genii",' said Fionnuala, her pretty-little-pink-nose expressing, in one fell swoop, her complete disdain for the stupidity of all little brothers, but especially for Albert.

'No, I mean that's genies you're describing,' said Albert, getting a little bit annoyed.

'Then you mean, "those are genii",' said Fionnuala with a sigh.

'Don't you tell me what I mean! What I mean is that's genies you're describing!' shouted Albert. He was very annoyed now.

'All right,' said Fionnuala. 'I know what you mean. Magicians are very like genii to look at, but genii are only made of smoke ...'

'Yes, yes, and live in lamps, I know,' said Albert, who really did know all about genies.

'Yes,' said Fionnuala, 'and live in lamps. Magicians are very like genii, except that they're made of real flesh and blood.'

When she said 'flesh and blood' she purred very slowly and made her eyes into slits and stretched the words out so that Albert would get the full effect of *raw* flesh with *fresh* blood dripping out of it. She was imagining an arm torn off at the elbow with sinews and all sorts of disgusting stringy bits hanging out of it, like the roots when one of your baby teeth comes out. Albert was imagining a pound of steak wrapped up in greaseproof paper in a butcher's shop.

'And what do they do?' asked Albert. His voice sounded very far away now and when Fionnuala looked over she saw that he was talking from underneath the bedclothes. She smiled to herself.

'Well ...' she said, 'sometimes they turn people into frogs.'

She did her usual backwards somersault into the top bunk, as she did every night, and she overshot, as she did every night, and slid down the gap between the bed and the wall and landed beside Albert.

'Willyageddoff!' Albert shouted. Naturally, being under the bedclothes, he hadn't seen Fionnuala taking off and her landing took him completely by surprise. His nerves were in a bad enough state with the description she was giving him of the magician, and a chubby, dopey, thaveless, big sister landing on top of him out of the blue was the last straw.

'Use the ladder, Fionnuala!' he growled.

'You're useless at somersaults! Even your nose is better at doing somersaults than you are! I don't know why you try ...'

'And I don't know whether I should tell you any more about magicians, Albert,' Fionnuala hissed, climbing up the ladder. She had one of her faces on and she was absolutely smarting from Albert's attack.

'I bet you've got one of your faces on!' said Albert from beneath the bedclothes.

That decided it. There had never been very much doubt about it, but now Fionnuala was going to scare the wits out of Albert, really scare the wits out of him – oh yes, she was! She was going to fix Albert good and proper.

'Hmmm ...' said Fionnuala, her pretty-little-pink-nose managing, all on its own, the somersault the rest of her could never hope for. 'I think, after all, I'd better not tell you the rest ... you're too young and it might frighten you and then you wouldn't be able to sleep, and that would make Mum cross ...' She was back to her extremely-grown-up voice.

'Tell me! I'm not frightened, honest,' said Albert.

'Augh no, Albert ... really, you're much too young to hear the rest ...' Now she was putting on the deeply-concerned-and-caring voice *as well as* the extremely-grown-up voice, *and* she was telling him he was too young. That was waving a red rag at a bull.

'AAAY YAMMINT TOO YOUNG!' hissed Albert.

'Come out from under the bedclothes then,' said Fionnuala. She'd got him there, and she was loving it. 'Are you sure you want to hear this?' Boy, was she an expert at Getting At Albert.

'YES!' said Albert. 'Right, go on! I'm out!'

'Well, sometimes they change themselves into snakes or dragons and then they hiss and breathe fire, and the smell of their breath is awful, and they spread ashes all over the place and they grow to the size of the room and they hiss and they puff and they grow to the size of the house and they hiss and they puff more and they grow to the size of the shopping centre and they devastate all the houses in front of them ...'

'What does devastate mean?' said a faraway voice.

'COME OUT FROM UNDER THOSE CLOTHES!' said Fionnuala. 'It means destroy, but never mind! I haven't come to the really bad bit yet. Guess what their Main Thing to do is?'

'What?' asked Albert.

'I'm not telling you unless you stay out!' said Fionnuala.

'Right! Right! Right!' said Albert, pulling the clothes from over his head again. 'WILLYA GEDDON WIVITT?'

Fionnuala's voice became very quiet. 'They appear in a cloud of smoke and red sparks and they kidnap boys, especially wee boys about seven, which is the perfect age for them, and they take them away to a foreign land that is all desert and absolutely crawling with snakes and scorpions and rats and tarantulas, and they lock them up in caves, full of gold and precious stones and other kinds of treasure, millions of miles away from their mums and dads and ...' Fionnuala was really getting warmed up now, and her voice was getting louder and louder.

'Don't tell me any more!' came Albert's voice from beneath the clothes again.

'Will you two get to sleep, NOW!' Dad's voice came from the bottom of the stairs.

'Sorry, Dad!' shouted Fionnuala. 'We're going to sleep right now!'

But Fionnuala knew that she'd done it and that *she* might be going to sleep, but Albert definitely wasn't. Poor Albert, he wouldn't sleep a wink tonight.

Fionnuala got cosy and yawned. She stretched, snuggled, turned up her pretty-little-pink-nose and settled, with a smile of satisfaction, for the night.

CHAPTER 5

The Walking Saint

POOR OLD ALBERT. He *didn't* sleep a wink that night. It wasn't how Fionnuala had described the magician that worried him. He knew perfectly well that magicians didn't look like that (it was genies that looked like that), but he couldn't get the thought of those blasted tarantulas out of his mind.

Albert hated spiders. He hated spiders as much as he hated spaghetti, well, almost as much as he hated spaghetti. He didn't hate *small* spiders, though, the ones you got around the house. They were all right. In fact, they were wildlife, and sometimes, if they were small, he would keep them in a matchbox as pets. They were brilliant for taking to school and frightening the girls with. Then there were the bigger, blacker ones that you got in the bath. Mum always said that they meant money – whatever she meant by that. It didn't matter to Albert whether they meant money or not – he didn't like them. He always made sure that you didn't get a big, black spider and an Albert in the bath at the same time. But the great big hairy ones, the ones you saw on TV, the ones you had to keep in big glass boxes, those were the ones that gave Albert the screaming, howling heebie-jeebies. And that Fionnuala knew it! That was why she had mentioned them in the first place. She'd be sorry!

When he came down to breakfast, Albert was on eggs.

'Good morning, Albert!' said Mum cheerfully. 'How would you like your eggs?'

'Scrambled, please, Mum,' said Albert, without much enthusiasm. He was feeling so bad he would probably not even have been enthusiastic about beans on toast, that was how bad he was feeling.

The Twins, the scourge of the household, was sitting in his high chair trying to open the Detergents, Drugs, Mousetraps, Medicines and Other Dangers to Children cupboard.

The Twins probably had a real name, but Albert had forgotten what it was. He never called him anything but The Twins – well actually he did, he called him lots of other things, but not when Mum or Dad was there. They usually allowed him to be called The Twins, in fact Dad had invented the name because he was so much trouble you got the feeling he could be in two places at once, and he definitely caused enough trouble for two. The Twins was having a problem. He hated being in his high chair and now his straps were holding him back so that he could hardly even reach the cupboard door. He started to fiddle with the safety clip.

'Eggs Bénédict, Eggs Florentine? Egg mayonnaise?' Mum went on.

'No, Mum, just scrambled, please,' said Albert. The woman thought of nothing but cooking! It was impossible to get through to her. By now Andy – yes, Albert remembered, that was The Twins' real name – Andy, scourge of the household, had managed to undo the safety clip of his straps and was pushing them off his shoulders. He had a look of terrible concentration on his face and he was singing to himself – probably some sort of battle hymn.

'I could do you a very nice *oeuf-en-cocotte*. It would be no trouble at all ...' said Mum.

'No, Mum, honestly, Mum, just scrambled eggs, honestly, that's all I want,' Albert said.

The Twins had escaped from his straps and from the seat of his high chair and was standing on his tiptoe, stretching as high as he could to

reach the handle of the D.D.M.M.O.D.C. cupboard. He looked like one of those men pushing out a boat while trying to stay on the land themselves. He was still singing to himself.

'Oh, very well, Albert, but if you don't eat, you know what will happen to you,' said Mum, 'and think of the wee-starving-children-in-the-Third-World.'

Albert thought to himself that it was probably the amount of food that his mother went through that had the Third World in the state it was in. She used enough rice in one week to feed the whole of India for a month. And here she was, worrying about Albert starving, while her other son, The Twins, was on the verge of committing suicide trying to open the D.D.M. M.O.D.C. cupboard – and heaven knows what he would get at if he managed to open that door without killing himself! It didn't bear thinking about. And if his mother wasn't going to think about it, then Albert wasn't going to think about it either. Albert had troubles of his own. He was thinking about what was going to happen to him whether he ate his breakfast or not. He had just two days to get out of going to see this horrible magician in school. How on earth was he going to do it?

He was so absorbed in his thoughts that he hardly noticed that The Twins' boat had gone out. The baby, the scourge of the household, *had* managed to get the door of the D.D.M. M.O.D.C. cupboard open, grabbed a bottle of fabric conditioner and pushed himself back on to the shelf of his high chair. At this very moment he was sitting on the shelf unscrewing the top of the bottle. He was probably wondering what the big black 'X' just above the words 'Poison: Keep Out of Reach of Children' meant. The Twins was dicing with death and singing his battle hymn: 'Bottom, bottom, bottom, bum bum de bum bum ...'

Now that was a thought, thought Albert, who

had noticed the big black 'X' too. He could poison himself. On the other hand he could save himself a lot of bother and just eat Mum's dinners for the rest of the week. That ought to do the trick.

'Bottom, bottom, bottom, bum bum de bum bum ...' sang The Twins.

'What is that child singing about?' asked Mum as she came back to the table carrying a plate.

'Bottoms,' said Albert, 'but he really means "bottles" ...'

'Here you are, Albert,' said Mum, 'scrambled eggs ...'

'Oh no!' said Albert, putting his hands over his eyes.

The Twins had managed to get the top off the bottle of fabric conditioner and was putting it up to his mouth. Mum still hadn't noticed.

Oh no ... thought Albert.

'Scrambled eggs *archiduchesse*!' Mum said,

setting the plate down in front of Albert.

Oh no, thought Albert. He opened one eye when he heard the plate being set on the table. It could have been worse. All he had to do was take the asparagus off the top, pick out the mushrooms and a few pieces of ham and he would be left with a fairly reasonable plate of scrambled eggs. In fact, he mightn't even take the ham out of it.

'I've been thinking, Mum,' he said, getting ready to apply the fork. Just as the fork touched the asparagus there was an unmerciful screech.

'Andy!'

Albert jumped and knocked against the plate. The plate hit the floor. The Twins jumped and caught the flap of his Babygro on the handle of the cupboard door. The fabric conditioner bottle hit the floor. Mum jumped and caught The Twins before he hit the floor. She was the one who had screeched.

'Why didn't you tell me what Andy was

doing?' she yelled, unhooking him from the D.D.M.M.O.D.C. cupboard door. 'Andy was dicing with death!'

'Sorry, Mum, I was thinking ...' said Albert.

'Were you, Albert?' said Mum, as she went back to the sink to dice an aubergine, or eggplant, with a little more energy than was really necessary. Bits of aubergine, or eggplant, were flying all over the kitchen. Mum was obviously thinking about Albert.

'I was, Mum,' said Albert, scraping scrambled egg, asparagus, ham and now aubergine, or eggplant, back on to his plate.

'What were you thinking, Albert?' asked Mum.

'This magician ...' said Albert.

'What magician?' asked Mum between gritted teeth. She was reaching for her *Book of Quick, Cheap and Healthy Continental Family Favourite Suppers for Weightwatchers with a Microwave on a Budget*. Not much chance of beans on toast tonight, Albert thought in passing.

'The magician who's supposed to be coming to school on Thursday,' said Albert.

'Yes?' said Mum. 'What about him?'

It was the thought of the Third World that had done it. 'Well,' said Albert, 'fifty pence is an awful lot of money, and I was thinking of all those poor-starving-people-in-the-Third-World that you were talking about last night, and I thought that if it was all right with you I might give my fifty pence to charity.'

'What fifty pence, Albert?' asked Mum.

'The fifty pence it costs to go in to see the magician,' explained Albert slowly. 'You know, the fifty pence you gave to Fionnuala to give to the headmaster ...'

'Right, right,' said Mum. 'Goodness, Albert, that's very thoughtful of you.'

If she only knew, thought Albert, just how thoughtful it was.

'You're a walking saint!' Mum continued.

I've done it! thought Albert, setting his plate of scrambled eggs back on the table. I've done it! I've done it! I've done it! And he grabbed his schoolbag and absolutely floated out the kitchen door.

'Wait, Albert! Your lunch. It's quiche Lorraine!' Mum shouted.

'Real men don't eat quiche, Mum!' Albert shouted back. 'Don't worry, I'll get crisps and orange at school. And my name's not Lorraine, it's Albert! Bye!' And a very happy Albert slammed the front door.

He was walking on air, and all the way from the front door of his house to the gates of the school Albert sang to himself, 'Dum doo dickey doo dum doo dickey dee, no magician, dum, no magician, dum, no magician for me; dum doo dickey doo dum doo dickey dee no magician, dum, no magician, no magician for me!'

CHAPTER 6

Jelly Beans on Stair-rods?

ALBERT FLOATED THROUGH SCHOOL all day. He didn't have a worry in the world. Even Fionnuala, try as she might, and she did try – her pretty-little-pink-nose was sore with all the acrobatics it was doing – couldn't put him into a bad mood. She spotted him at lunchtime. He was just starting to blow up an empty crisp bag when she crept up behind him.

'Did you not get any lunch?' she said quietly, sticking the forefinger of each hand into his sides.

Normally he would have blown up too, but he

just took the crisp bag down from his mouth and said with a smile, 'I got crisps and orange.'

She couldn't believe it. She tried another trick. 'You should taste this quiche Lorraine, Albert, it's ...' She was about to say 'mouth-watering', when Albert interrupted her.

'It's rotten,' he said. 'And don't call me Lorraine, my name's Albert!'

'You're right,' said Fionnuala, her pretty-little-pink-nose drooping. 'It is rotten.'

Albert was in such a good mood that she decided there was no point in trying to annoy him, so she gave up. She just didn't understand it! After the story she had told him last night, he should have been quaking in his boots.

'And what has you in such a good mood?' she asked, her pretty-little-pink-nose climbing back up her face and her hands on her hips.

'Nothing,' said Albert. 'Have you seen the old Chicken?'

'No,' said Fionnuala.

'I need a word with him,' said Albert, smiling a self-satisfied smile as he floated off to interview the headmaster. 'Dum doo dickey doo dum doo dickey dee ...'

The Chicken was out in the playground, holding a newspaper under one of his wings, which he had folded behind his back, pecking at a group of girls and scratching one of his brown brogues in the dust and screenings.

'Please, sir, Mr Curry,' Albert said.

'Yes, Lorraine?' said the headmaster.

'It isn't Lorraine, sir, it's me, Albert,' said Albert.

'*Bwook!* ... Sorry, Albert, I thought you were ... *bwook* ... Lorraine,' the headmaster apologised.

Albert accepted his apology gracefully. He was in a good mood. The Chicken would be in a good mood too – he had obviously eaten his lunch. 'That's all right, sir, I want to ask you something ...' and he took the headmaster aside and explained slowly and in great detail, so that he could not fail to understand, to the third button up from the bottom of the headmaster's something-to-do-with-cows-coloured waistcoat, about Mum and the poor-wee-starving-children -in-the-Third-World and how exactly he planned to do his bit for them if that was all right with the headmaster, of course.

'*Bwook*!' said the headmaster, flabber-gasted. 'Of course it is! My goodness ... *bwook* ... you're a walking saint!'

The headmaster walked off towards his office, pecking the ground occasionally to pick up a crisp bag in a distracted sort of way, scratching his balding head with his wing-tip and looking slightly worried. Albert floated off in the opposite direction, humming, 'Dum doo dickey doo dum doo dickey dee ...' and he hummed all the way through school and all the way home and all the way upstairs to change for dinner and all the way downstairs again, where he met Dad coming in from work.

'That's a shocking day! It's raining stair-rods!' said Dad, rubbing his hands together. 'What's for dinner, Albert?'

Albert liked his Dad. You always knew where you stood with him. But every evening when he came in from work, he would rub his hands together and ask what was for dinner. What Albert could never understand was how he managed to be so cheerful and pretend he was looking forward to it. He couldn't really be looking forward to it, could he? Of course not!

'You look as if you're in a good mood, Albert,' Dad said. 'Is it beans?'

'Don't think so, Dad,' Albert replied, still smiling. 'Saw Mum being very violent with one of those purple things this morning.'

'Purple things?' asked Dad.

'Looks like a jelly bean on stair-rods,' said Albert. 'You know them ... horrible ... green plug at one end, eugh ...'

'Stair-rods?' asked Dad.

'Yes,' said Albert. 'You know ... for body-building ...'

'You mean steroids!' said Dad.

'That's what I said,' said Albert. 'Stair-rods.'

Dad gave up and sat down. He had had a hard enough day already. 'Jelly bean ... stair-rods ... horrible ... green plug ... aaah, you must mean an aubergine?' he said.

'So you think they're horrible too?' asked Albert, smiling again and thinking what a nice man his dad was and what good taste he had.

'No I do not, Albert,' said Dad.

'Doesn't really matter,' said Albert. 'I wasn't going to be able to eat it anyway.'

'Why not, Albert?' asked Dad, who really was a walking saint.

'Wildlife, Dad,' said Albert, looking serious for the first time since Dad had come in.

'Wildlife, Albert? What on earth has wildlife got to do with you and your dinner?' asked Dad.

'Well,' said Albert slowly. He could see he was going to have to explain this carefully to his dad. The headmaster was the same – in fact, Albert thought, all grown-ups are like that, a little bit slow. 'You know I like wildlife, Dad?'

'Yes,' said Dad, getting more and more baffled.

'Well, you know what a moose is, Dad?' asked Albert.

'Isn't it a Scottish mouse?' asked Dad.

'No, Dad,' said Albert, who didn't think daddies ought to try to be funny.

'Sorry, Albert,' said Dad. 'Only trying to be funny. It's a big deer, isn't it?'

'Yes, Daddy,' said Albert.

'Just like Mum!' said Dad.

Albert ignored him. For one thing, Mum was not big, but he couldn't be bothered to explain that. Fionnuala was coming down the stairs.

'And it's an endangered species,' Albert continued.

'Just like Mum!' said Fionnuala, squeezing past Albert. 'Excuse me!'

Albert excused her. She would never know how much Albert excused her! He rolled his eyes to heaven. This conversation was becoming impossible.

'Well, guess what Mum's making for dinner,' said Albert.

'This conversation is becoming impossible!' said Dad. 'I have been trying to find out for the past ten minutes what Mum's making for dinner.'

'Guess,' said Albert.

'I give up!' said Dad.

'Moussaka!' said Albert.

'Oh lovely!' said Dad. There he goes again, thought Albert, wondering once more how he managed it. 'But what on earth has that got to do with wildlife?'

'Well, you know what Mum's like about *real* beans and *real* spaghetti?' said Albert.

'Yes, Albert,' said Dad.

'If she's going to make *real* moussaka, she's going to use *real* moose!' said Albert. 'I can't eat wildlife, Dad, especially endangered species!'

'Don't be silly, Albert!' said Dad. 'Anyway, moussaka has nothing to do with moose. Aubergines and peppers and tomatoes and mince – no jelly beans, no steroids, no moose, no wildlife. But I'll tell you something: if you don't eat your dinner, *you'll* be an endangered species!'

'Dinner!' said Mum, carrying in a steaming casserole of moussaka.

'Eugh!' said Albert.

'Me hover beans!' said The Twins, who was already strapped into his high chair. Mum had put the little brass lock on it. Albert ignored him.

They all sat down at the table. Albert picked his way through his plate of moussaka. He put the tomatoes and mushrooms and aubergine and peppers and anything else he could recognise on one side of the plate, and he pushed all the dead moose to the other. Then he didn't eat either.

'Honestly, Albert, it's just ordinary mince!' said Dad.

'It's dead moose,' said Albert.

The Twins wasn't very keen on his either until he discovered that aubergine makes a wonderfully satisfying wet thwack when it is dropped on to tiles.

'Hover beans eugh!' he said, shovelling it over the side of his high chair.

Fionnuala stopped eating and picked some-thing from between her teeth. She rolled it between her finger and thumb for a moment, then wiped it off on to the side of her plate and wiped her finger on the front of her jersey.

'What's that?' asked Mum.

'I think it was a bit of bone,' said Fionnuala.

'Probably antler!' said Albert.

When dinner was over Dad helped Mum clear

the table then came back and sat down.

'I've got good news and bad news for you, Albert. Which do you want first?' said Dad.

'There is no such thing as a bad gnu,' said Albert. 'Gnus are wildlife!'

It was Dad's turn to ignore the joke, so Albert said, 'All right, give me the good gnus.' He was still feeling a little bit depressed by having had to sit in front of a plate of dead moose for the last twenty minutes.

'The good news is that Mum and I have been talking about you ...' said Dad.

'... and she thinks I'm starving, so she's going to make me beans on toast?' asked Albert, his eyes lighting up.

'No,' said Dad. 'Even better than that.'

'What?' asked Albert.

'Guess!' said Dad.

'Can't!' said Albert.

'Well, we've decided that it was so good of you to give up your fifty pence for the poor-starving-children-of-the-Third-World, that as a special treat we're going to give you fifty pence more so that you can go and see the magician anyway. Isn't that good?' said Dad.

When Albert came back down from the ceiling, Dad said, 'Do you want the bad news now?'

'Give it to me straight ...' said Albert.

'You can't eat the dessert,' said Dad.

'Typical!' said Albert. 'Why not?'

'Chocolate mousse!' said Dad.

CHAPTER 7

How to Address
a Cloud of Smoke

'MUM,' SAID ALBERT on Thursday morning, 'I think I'm going to have a baby ...'

'No, Albert, you're going to school,' said Mum.

It was a long shot. He didn't think she'd fall for it. He was far too thin, but he thought he'd better try it anyway. It was Albert's last resort. He just had to get out of going to see this magician.

Mum hadn't believed anything he'd tried in the past two days, and Albert had tried *everything*. He started with the measles, but Dad spotted that one right away and rubbed two or three of the spots off Albert's face with his finger. So then Albert went in for some diseases that were more exotic and whose symptoms were invisible: 'flu, sore stomach, sprains, strains, sore throat ... *everything*. None of them worked for more than half an hour. Albert had very suspicious parents.

For two whole days he ate every meal Mum cooked. He'd never done that before. It was the one thing that almost convinced his parents that Albert really was sickening for something. He thought it was bound to do the trick. If you ate everything Mum cooked, you were absolutely certain to catch something. When they had salmon – *salmon en croute* – on Wednesday night, Albert deliberately asked for an extra-large helping. He thought Mum had said salmon *uncooked*, and he knew there was salmonella about – Albert was no fool, though he felt like one when he saw the two parcels of salmon in flaky pastry he had to get through that night.

Now here it was, Thursday morning, and he had to keep trying right up to the end.

'Headache, Mum,' he said.

'School, Albert,' said Mum.

'Constipation, Mum,' said Albert.

'School, Albert,' said Mum.

'The humps?' said Albert.

'What?' said Mum.

'Oh mumps! I mean mumps,' said Albert.

'School, Albert,' groaned Mum.

'Torn ligament ...' said Albert.

'School, Albert ...' hissed Mum.

'*Migraine*?' asked Albert.

'*School!*' shouted Mum.

'DIARRHOEA!' shouted Albert.

'SCHOOL!' roared Mum.

Albert had been through all the ailments he knew, so there was nothing left for it. Albert went to school.

'Disappointed that your list of diseases didn't work, Albert?' asked Fionnuala on the way, her pretty-little-pink-nose so high in the air it was in danger of getting tangled up with the electricity wires. She had seen through most of his cunning plans over the past two days, and hadn't given him a moment's peace since.

'A trifle,' said Albert listlessly, remembering last night's dessert. He slung his schoolbag over his other shoulder. 'Now whydontya BUZZ OFF?'

Fionnuala reckoned she couldn't really add very much to Albert's present discomfort, so she did. She buzzdoff.

Alone now, walking to school, Albert mused. He didn't know he was musing, because even though he'd read the word – practically every book Albert had ever read had people musing in it – he'd never seen anybody actually doing it, but Albert was definitely musing. Wasn't it strange, he mused, how time could pass so quickly and seem so long at the same time? This

week had been both the longest and the short-est week of Albert's life so far. He had dreaded the thought of Thursday coming, but here it was anyway. Before he knew it, it would be breaktime ...'

🕐 🕐 🕐

Brrrrrrrrrrrrrrrrrrrrrrrrrrrrrrrrrrrrr!!!!!!!

It was breaktime.

Albert was sitting on the playground wall just beside the school gates, still trying desperately to think of some last way of getting out of going to see the magician. He was only vaguely aware of the noise of the other children in the playground. He was even less aware of a dim chug-chugging on the road behind him. It had been getting louder for some time.

Suddenly there were two very loud bangs and a cloud of smoke pulled up at the school gates with a screech, a shower of red sparks and a smell of burning oil. There was a final crabbed chug-chug.

'Excuse me, young man,' said the cloud of smoke.

Albert picked himself up from the ground, where he had dived for cover when he heard the two loud bangs. He rubbed the small, sharp stones out of his hands. He was very angry. He looked out the gate. The shower of red sparks had disappeared, but the smell of burning oil was getting stronger.

'Excuse me, young man,' the cloud of smoke said again. 'I'm sorry to bother you, but could you tell me if this is, in fact, as I suspect, the Mid-Ulster Academical Institution for the Education of the Bright, the Not-so-bright, the Prim, the Not-so-prim, the Proper and the Slightly Improper?'

'You mean St Michael's?' asked Albert, who was extremely bothered. He wondered if he should add 'sir'. He had never spoken to a cloud of smoke before.

'Precisely,' said the cloud of smoke.

'Yes,' said Albert, still not able to make up his mind.

'I thought it might be,' said the cloud of smoke. 'And would this be the Preparatory Department?'

'Yes, sir,' said Albert, just to be on the safe side. You never knew.

'Good!' said the cloud of smoke with a satisfied laugh. 'I knew I'd come to the right place.'

And as suddenly as it had come the cloud of smoke disappeared, leaving Albert face-to-face with a little old man and a big old motorbike.

CHAPTER 8

Mr McFerran

ALBERT BREATHED A SIGH OF RELIEF.
Clouds of smoke were one thing, but little old
men were another. Albert could deal with little
old men. Anybody who could deal with Albert's
little brother, The Twins, could deal with most
forms of human life and most forms of wildlife
as well.

Albert looked at the motorbike. All over the
back and around the sides it was loaded with
battered brown suitcases and cardboard boxes.
They were tied on with hairy, fraying bits of
string and old belts. The little old man had

taken off his battered black crash helmet. Unlike the pieces of string, he was not hairy, apart from just above his ears. His head was completely bald except for one long greasy stripe of hair that went right across his skull from one ear to the other.

He was beginning to untie some of his boxes and things were falling off the motorbike and all over the road. He was talking to himself all the time, muttering numbers and dates and strange words that Albert had never heard before. Mixed up with these Albert made out the word 'frog' or 'froggies' several times and the words 'dear boy'.

Every so often the little old man would break off from what he was doing and just giggle to himself. Each time he bent down to untie something, the stripe of greasy hair slipped from the top of his head and down on to his shoulder, and each time he straightened up the little old man pulled it back across the top of his head.

'I wonder, young man, if you would be good enough to lead me to the headmaster's office?' said the little old man, straightening up from a box and pulling the stripe of hair across his bald head again. He leaned over the school gates with his two arms hanging down. The cuffs of his white shirt were grey and scruffy and the sleeves of his coat were ragged, but Albert noticed that his hands were long and pale, nimble and delicate.

Albert had better things to do this breaktime than to direct this peculiar old buffer to the headmaster's office. He had to find a way out of seeing the magician, but he found himself saying, almost against his will, 'Of course ... certainly, sir.'

The little old man suddenly began to take off the dirty, belted, grey-green gabardine overcoat he was wearing, and Albert saw, to his surprise, that beneath it was a dinner jacket and bow tie. The bottoms of his baggy black trousers didn't

quite reach the tops of his big black boots. He draped the coat carefully over the saddle of the motorbike, which was now creaking and groaning like a central-heating boiler cooling down, adjusted his black bow tie and opened the school gate.

He seemed to be chewing something – something small, like a grain of rice – and he was humming a strange little tune to himself.

Albert took him to the headmaster's office, and just as they reached the door it opened and the headmaster came out.

'Ah, Mr Mc ... *bwook* ... Ferran!' said the headmaster. 'Lovely to see you again.'

'Headmaster!' said the little old man with one of his strange, high-pitched giggles.

'No difficulty getting here I hope?' the headmaster continued.

'None whatsoever, thank you, though when you visit as many schools as I do, it's easy to mix them up. This kind young gentleman confirmed that I had come to the right place,' said the little ragged man in his little squeaky voice.

'Yes ... *bwook* ... Albert,' said the headmaster, without, Albert thought, much enthusiasm. 'I suppose you'll be wanting some ... *bwook* ... help with your things, Mr Mc ... *bwook* ... Ferran?' he added.

'That would be lovely. I would be extremely grateful,' giggled the old man.

'Well, Albert here will help you for the time being, and I'll go and get a couple of big ... *bwook* ... strong boys. Will you help Mr Mc ... *bwook* ... Ferran with his ... *bwook* ... equipment, Albert?' asked the headmaster.

'Yes, sir,' said Albert. He was very cross with The Chicken. He hadn't time to help this old man. There were other things that needed his urgent attention. There was a blasted magician coming to this school in a matter of minutes and Albert had to find a way to escape. But there was nothing for it except to do what he was told.

The magician would have to wait. He followed the little old ragged man across the playground and out the school gates. The little old man twitched his head and slicked back his flap of hair and giggled and talked to himself.

Albert shoved his hands into his pockets, kicked at the sharp grey stones and muttered to himself.

CHAPTER 9

A Cultural Attaché Case

IT DID NOT SURPRISE ALBERT at all when no big ... *bwook* ... strong boys turned up. That was just Albert's luck. For the next fifteen minutes Albert and the ragged little man carried box after box and lugged suitcase after suitcase into the assembly hall and up on to the stage. The little man giggled and laughed and hummed and told silly jokes and made funny noises. Albert thought he was very odd, but nice too in a peculiar sort of way.

Strangely enough, Albert was very good with older people. When he had to go down to

Janice's house after school with Miriam and Therese, he always made an excuse to visit Granny Hunt three doors up and have a cup of tea and a chat with her. Albert regarded this as doing his civic duty. It had nothing to do with the chocolate biscuits Granny Hunt kept in a tin beside the cooker. Albert could *talk* to her. He couldn't talk to this little man, though. They were both too busy.

Eventually, Albert and the little old man had brought everything in except for one big suitcase. Albert went ahead of the old man this time, and he lifted the suitcase off the back of the motorbike. It was the oldest and most battered case of the lot and was covered with yellowing labels and stickers from all over the world. Albert got a chance to read some of them as he waited for the little old man to catch up. One said DARJEELING HAS IT TO A T! And another said DON'T FORGET YOUR BAGHDAD, and another SUNNY PRESTATYN

– Albert wasn't sure if that was an advertisement for a seaside resort or an instruction telling little boys how to open the case.

The old man had certainly been to some strange and far-flung places. There were two big red labels on top of the case. One said THIS SIDE UP and the other said FRAGILE! HANDLE WITH CARE. They looked very important.

'I'll take that one, thank you!' said the little old man when he reached the motorbike.

'It's no trouble at all, really,' said Albert, who by now had realised that it was too late to do any serious thinking anyway; breaktime was almost over.

The old man seemed to hesitate a little, then suddenly made up his mind, jerked his head to one side, hair flying all over the place, giggled and said, 'Oh, very well then, if you're sure?'

'Absolutely certain, sir,' said Albert, and the old man stepped back and let Albert pick up the case.

'Be careful, now,' said the little old man. 'The contents of that case are particularly delicate!' And he giggled to himself again, put his hand into his jacket pocket and popped a handful of uncooked rice into his mouth. They set off across the playground, Albert leading the way, tugging the very big, very heavy suitcase, the little old man following, giggling and talking to himself and spraying the playground with grains of uncooked rice.

Suddenly, halfway across the playground a voice said, 'Go easy with me now!'

The voice came out of the suitcase! Albert's hair stood on end. Was there somebody inside the suitcase? A prisoner? A hostage? It *was* heavy, Albert thought, but not that heavy. Albert looked around. Perhaps one of the terrible Ps was playing a trick on him? There was nobody nearby. There was a collection of Primary Three girls playing Queenio beside the wall, but there wasn't a boy in sight. The only person near enough to have had any influence was the little old man, and it couldn't have been him. Albert had been keeping his eye on him. He was standing beside Albert now, still chewing and spluttering rice, giggling to himself and looking at the school doors. Albert decided he must have imagined it. His nerves were on edge, that was all it was. That *must* be it.

'Do *not* swing me!' said the suitcase.

Albert jumped and started walking again, still looking to left and right to see if there was anybody there.

'*Stop it!* You're making me dizzy!' hissed the suitcase.

'Excuse me, sir, did you say something?' asked Albert.

'No, I don't think so,' said the little old man, who was giggling so much now that his shoulders were shaking, and not only was he spluttering uncooked rice from his mouth, but it was starting to fly out of the pockets of his crumpled dinner jacket. It was as if he were living in his own personal hailstorm.

By now they'd reached the door of the assembly hall and were moving towards the stage, where the rest of the boxes and cases had been set down.

'Now put me down gently! *Gently!*' said the suitcase.

The little man was absolutely chortling now. Albert's eyes were like saucers.

'Thank you,' said the suitcase as Albert set it down. 'I have travelled the world over, from Darjeeling to Singapore, from New York to Timbuktu. I have been shunted by coolies, hefted by stevedores, picked up by picadors, unloaded by urchins and manhandled by lascars, but I have never ... never ... never had as rough a time as this!'

Albert was having a pretty rough time, too.

He looked over at the little old man. It definitely was not him. His mouth was still almost full of rice, and he started to chortle again as soon as the case had stopped talking.

'Did you hear anything, sir?' asked Albert.

'Nothing, dear boy, nothing – except perhaps the chirping of the housemartins on the tele-graph wires, the croaking of the little froggies in the playground ...' said the little old man.

Housemartins on the wires? Little froggies in the playground? What on earth was this man talking about? The only wildlife in the play-ground was the girls out of Primary Three. Albert decided the old man must be mad.

'Now, that's the lot,' said the little old man. 'I am deeply indebted to you. Can I give you a tip?'

This is more like it, thought Albert, whose savings had been in a very bad state ever since he had decided to leave home and had bought himself a sleeping bag.

'Oh, please, think nothing of it, not at all, I wouldn't dream of, I couldn't possibly accept ...' said Albert, holding out his hand.

'Very well then,' said the little old man with a giggle. 'Don't believe everything you hear – that's my tip to you!' And then he began to giggle again, and he began to chortle, and he giggled and he chortled and he chortled and he giggled until the rice started to fly all over the place once more, and the stripe of hair flapped and swung, and the chortle turned into a laugh and the laugh turned into a deafening roar.

'Eey-hay-hay-hay, eey-hoo-hoo-hoo, uhh-uhh-a-hey-hoo!' went the little old man. Then he pushed the stripe of greasy hair back over the top of his bald head, and, for the first time since he met him, as the old man disappeared round the corner into the corridor, Albert, standing there with his hand out, noticed what he was wearing ...

CHAPTER 10

Guess What ...

... A SINGLE, SMALL, GOLD EARRING.

It couldn't be, thought Albert. But what about the earring? And the body in the suitcase? Albert put his hands in his pockets.

No, it couldn't be, he thought again. But it *could* be! No, it couldn't. The Chicken knew him. He had seen him before, so he must have been at the school before. He had called him 'Mr Mc ... *bwook* ... Ferran'. The magician was called The Great Gazebo – you couldn't have a magician called Mr McFerran, now could you? It was far too ordinary ...

Could be him in disguise, thought Albert. The Great Gazebo could be an assumed name, and what about the laugh? Albert could still hear it ringing in his ears, that terrible, horrible laugh: Eey-hay-hay-hay, eey-hoo-hoo-hoo, uhh-uhh-hey-hoo! Even after he stopped remembering the laugh, Albert's ears continued to ring. He could feel his heart pumping and the blood rushing from it right through his body and thumping into his brain.

If chubby, crabby, Miss Smarty-Pants Fionnuala were right about any of these things – and Miss Fionnuala and that pretty-little-pink-nose of hers were right about most things – then maybe she was right about the rest. Maybe the voice from the suitcase was a little boy of seven that the magician had kidnapped from some other school ...

Suddenly the ringing in Albert's ears became absolutely deafening.

Brrrrrrrrrrrrrrrrrrrrrrrrrrrrrr!

He was standing right below the school bell. It had just gone. It was the end of break. It was almost the end of Albert. This day was going from bad to worse. Albert was going to class.

Before he knew what was happening the bell rang again and the teacher said, 'Right, boys and girls, in line, please. We're going to the assembly hall to see the magician. Statues!'

When teacher said 'Statues!' you had to stand perfectly still and not move a muscle.

'OK,' said teacher. 'Let's go!'

'Oh brilliant!' said the rest of the boys and girls.

Oh blast! thought Albert.

And off they marched to the assembly hall.

He sat in his usual place between the two Peters, except that he didn't feel as if he was sitting. He felt he was floating about five centimetres above his chair. His heart was still thumping and his hands were shaking. He felt time was going very, very quickly and very slowly at the same time. He felt as if he wasn't really there, but was watching everything that was happening as if it were on TV.

Albert was convinced of two things. First, he was sure that the little old man he had met at the gates of the playground *was* the magician, and second, he was sure the magician had already decided that Albert was to be his victim.

Then Albert had a great idea. Well, it wasn't a really great idea, but it was the best he could think of. He decided that he would keep his eyes shut tight all through the show. It was something he always did at the dentist's. He just sat down on that awful big leather chair, shut his eyes and opened his mouth and sang inside his head. It worked. You never knew what kind of gruesome pliers or needles or scrapers or pokers or chisels or hammers or drills the dentist was using, and you didn't feel a thing. Well, you almost didn't feel a thing. Then Albert had another good idea. Instead of singing inside his head, he would pray. He would pray like mad. He shut his eyes tight and started to pray. And he prayed like mad.

'Boys and ... *bwook* ... girls,' The Chicken began, 'I know how ... *bwook* ... much you've all been looking forward to this ... *bwook* ... moment ...'

Albert broke off from praying like mad just long enough to think to himself that The Chicken had absolutely no idea how he had looked forward to this ... *bwook* ... moment, then he went straight back to praying like mad.

'... so, without further a ... *bwook* ... ado, let me introduce our very special visitor. Boys and girls, a big ... *bwook* ... hand for The Great Gazebo!'

The boys and girls all started to clap and cheer, then the clapping and cheering died down and the room went very quiet. Albert heard the curtains open, then there were a few more seconds of silence, followed by an ear-splitting explosion. Albert jumped, all the boys and girls gasped and then started to laugh and cheer and clap again. Albert heard a voice and the applause petered out again. Albert got as low down in his seat as he could.

'I thankah yeough! I thankah yeough!'

It was! It was, it was, it *was*! It was the voice of the little old man, and it went on, 'Ladies and gentlemen, I am so pleased to be here with you today. I hope you enjoy my ... little ... hay-hay-hay ... performance!'

It is! It is, it is, it IS! thought Albert. Oh blast!

'Before I start,' the voice of the magician continued, 'I would like to say that there is one very important person in this room. It is one of you. It is someone whom I would like to take with me ...' the voice giggled, '... on a little adventure! On a voyage, let us say, on a journey into the land of mystery ... the land of the unknown!'

It's me! It's me! thought Albert. Oh blast! Blast, blast, blast, blast, blast! And he squeezed his eyes tighter than ever.

The next thing that Albert heard was the sound of metal wheels moving across the stage.

'What's happening, Peetie?' he whispered.

'He's just wheeled out a big blue box!' The words came from both sides of Albert, a different voice in each ear. He thought he was going mad. Then he remembered that he had one Terrible Peter on each side of him.

'Describe it to me!' he said.

'It's blue,' said his right ear.

'It's got stars on it,' said his left ear.

'It's got a kind of a door in it,' said his right ear.

'Is it on its bottom or on its side?' said Albert. He needed to know.

'Hard to say,' said his left ear. 'Depends. Depends on what you mean by bottom.'

'Depends on which way you look at it,' said the other ear.

'Whichever way it is, the bit that's on the floor is the bottom,' said his right ear.

'Look,' said Albert. 'Is it standing straight up or lying on its back?'

'What do you want to know that for?' asked his left ear.

'Just tell me ... *please* ...' said Albert. If it were lying on its back Albert was safe ... for the time being anyway.

'It's lying on its back,' said his right ear.

Albert was so relieved that he let out a sigh.

'Hold on a second, though,' said his left ear. 'He's moving it.'

There was a grunt from the stage.

'Standing straight up,' said his right ear.

'Oh, no!' groaned Albert. The reason he wanted to know was very simple. If the big long box had been lying on its back it would have meant that the magician was going to saw somebody in half, and magicians always sawed ladies in half, and that would have been fine for Albert. In fact, he had the very lady in mind. But if it were standing straight up it meant that he was going to make somebody ... well, you know what, don't you?

'Pray silence, if you please,' said the high-pitched voice from the stage. 'I will now step down from the stage and walk among you to seek out my ... little friend,' said the magician. And then he laughed. 'Eey-hay-hay-hay, eey-hoo-hoo-hoo, uhh-uhh-hey-hoo!'

You could feel the silence in the hall.

Oh blow! Oh blow, blow, blow, blast, blast! went Albert.

Then the footsteps started. They were the heavy footsteps of the magician's big black boots, and they creaked and they squeaked, and the creaking and the squeaking got louder and louder and closer and closer until it was right beside Albert's row. Then it stopped. Albert's heart was in his mouth. Then the creaking and squeaking started again and began to move slowly away from Albert's row.

Oh thank you! Thank you, *thank you,*

THANK YOU! thought Albert. The footsteps continued to move away, slowly, slowly, and Albert was so relieved that for the first time in about five minutes he breathed out.

But he had to be sure. He had to check. He turned carefully around and opened one eye. He had been right. There, about two metres away he saw the back of a black dinner jacket and above it a hat like a lampshade with a flowerpot on top. And suddenly, before he knew what was happening, the magician had spun round and was staring right at Albert.

'Aaah-haaah!' hissed the magician. 'And here he is!'

And then he laughed. 'Eey-hay-hay-hay, eey-hoo-hoo-hoo, uhh-uhh-hey-hoo!'

And Albert shut his eyes tight again and thought, Blast! Blast, blast blast ...

CHAPTER 11

Hokus Pokus Jess-a-locus ...

'EARLIER TODAY,' SAID THE MAGICIAN, moving across Albert's row and grasping his hand, 'I promised this young man a tip, and when I gave him my tip he looked a little disappointed. Ever since then I have been asking myself what I might do that would not disappoint him.' Now the magician was leading Albert, whose eyes were still shut tight, out into the aisle and up on to the stage, talking as he went. 'This is what I have decided upon.'

Albert's knees were knocking. Nobody was laughing. There was a deathly hush in the hall.

'What is your name, young man?' asked the magician, and before Albert could answer 'Albert', he went on, 'It is Albert, isn't it?'

'Albert, sir,' said Albert.

'Good ... good. Now, Albert, hold out your hand,' said the magician.

Albert held out his hand, trying very, very hard to stop it shaking.

'A little higher, if you please,' said the magician.

Albert held it higher. His eyelids were flickering and there were coloured clouds passing round and round his eyeballs, and his ears were ringing.

'But no!' said the magician, as if he had just thought of something. 'I have just thought of something.'

So had Albert.

Blast! Albert thought.

'I was going to give you a tip – and I still am – but before I do ... are you a good traveller, my little Albert? Are you a well-travelled Albert? Do you *enjoy* travelling?'

The furthest Albert had ever been was Belfast, which was far enough for him. He tried to answer, but his throat was so dry no words came out of his mouth, so he just shook his head.

'That's a pity. You don't like to travel, eh?' asked the magician. 'Eh? Eh? Eey-hay-hay-hay, eey-hoo-hoo-hoo, uhh-uhh-a-hey hoo!'

Albert kept shaking his head frantically. He felt the magician taking the hand he was holding up in his own delicate, nimble-fingered hand. The magician's hand was as cold as ice. Albert's hand was sweating. When the magician's hand touched his, he felt the sweat on his hand go cold. The magician brought Albert's hand down.

'Follow me, please,' he said, and Albert felt himself being led across the stage.

Oh no! Albert groaned. He stood very still

while the magician turned him round and kept on talking to the audience.

'This may look, to you, like a perfectly ordinary box ...' the magician let go of Albert's hand and swirled the box, which must have been on some sort of wheels or castors, banged each side with his fist, then opened and closed the door at the front '... it is, in fact, not merely a box. It is a Time/Space Disrupter. Watch. We place The Subject in the box ...' He guided Albert, who didn't so much walk as shuffle gently into the box. 'Excellent! Just the right size! Are you quite comfortable?'

The Subject didn't say anything.

'Good!' said the magician. 'And now we close the door of the box.'

The hinges creaked and Albert felt himself suddenly getting very warm and his breath bouncing back at him. He opened his eyes for the first time in what seemed like about a year and a half. He might as well not have

bothered. He was in complete darkness. Then he heard the magician say, '*Zezubjet iznow, booing vransp ...*'

At least that's what it sounded like to Albert. He could hardly make out a single word. The magician went on talking for ages. Albert prayed like mad. Then everything went completely white and Albert thought something terrible had happened. But he found he was staring out into the eyes of the magician who was staring back at him, smiling and giggling. He must have opened the top half of the door of the box, Albert thought.

'Yes, The Subject is perfectly comfortable,' the magician said in a loud voice and slammed the door shut and everything went dark again.

Had Albert been somewhere else, which he wasn't, he would have objected strongly to being called 'The Subject'. Albert, if you remember, didn't like people talking about him as if he wasn't there. There was more of the booming talk Albert couldn't understand, followed by four great thumps on each of the sides of the box and immediately after that Albert *wasn't* there.

I can tell you what the boys and girls in the audience saw – they saw the magician banging with his magic wand on each side of the box. Then Albert heard him saying the magic words, *'Okus bokus essa mokus, ire and aurus a loada dopus!'* And as he heard them they seemed to get smaller and smaller, and weaker and weaker. It was just as if he had jumped off a cliff and somebody at the top of the cliff was shouting after him, 'DON'T jump Alberrrrrrrrrttt ...' The audience heard what the magician actually said. He said, *'Hokus pokus jess-a-locus, tyrannosaurus diplodocus!'*

CHAPTER 12

The Return of Albert

OUT OF THE BLACKNESS there was a swirling of stars that turned into black spiders and crawled quickly across the whitening sky. Wriggling worms of light, blue and green and red and yellow, flickered and streaked across Albert's tightly-shut eyes. His head was whirling and spinning and flying. Zig-zags like sergeant's stripes twinkled and shimmered at the edges of his vision. His ears whooshed and hissed and twinkled and crackled. It seemed to last for ages.

Far away on the stage of the assembly hall the

magician had wheeled a rack of swords out of the wings. The *William Tell Overture* played frantically (if you are an intellectual you'll know it as the music from *The Lone Ranger*) and the magician thrust sabre after sabre, scimitar after scimitar, cutlass after cutlass, épée after épée, rapier after rapier into the box, then, just as the music ended, the magician dashed round and started opening the locks one after the other, flung open the doors and, with a flourish, showed the audience that the inside of the box was completely empty. Not an Albert in sight.

'Eh, *voilá!*' The magician held out his hands and smiled.

The audience gasped. It had been a gasping kind of afternoon for them. The magician noticed one big girl whose face had been getting whiter and whiter and who had been wriggling and fidgeting all through this part of the show. She couldn't contain herself any longer. She jumped up from the middle of the crowd and shouted, 'Hey!'

It was, of course, Fionnuala.

Suddenly the doors at the back of the assembly hall got an unmerciful thump and burst open. The audience all jumped up and swung around, hopping up and down to see over each other. Light streamed in from the back of the hall, and, standing with his back to them, silhouetted against the sunshine, was the small, baffled figure of an Albert. *Their* Albert. There was a great big cheer and Albert swung round.

'Albert!' they all shouted, and back on stage the magician, smiling from ear to ear, said again, 'Eh, *voilá!* Come to me, my little friend!'

Albert, not surprisingly, hesitated for a moment. He was dazed, and not quite sure if he wanted to see the magician again. But the crowd clapped and cheered and the magician smiled and held out his hands and, magically, a causeway opened up among the pupils and they parted like the Red Sea in front of the Israelites to let Albert get to the stage. So Albert licked his lips and took a deep breath and puffed out his chest and marched through his people as if he were Moses, and straight up on to the stage, where he confronted the magician.

'Now,' said the magician, 'hold out your hand and I will give you that tip, my brave little friend!'

So Albert, staring confidently at the audience, held out his hand.

'That's right,' said the magician. 'Now, don't be afraid. That's right, that's right ... a little higher ... higher ... higher ...' As he spoke, his voice, like Albert's hand, was getting higher, higher, higher. He lifted Albert's small, warm hand with his own long, cool, nimble fingers. The touch made a shiver run down Albert's spine again, and all the old dread came flooding back.

Then there was a moment's complete silence before he whispered, 'That's perfect!'

Albert was leaning away from the magician. He was worried again. He looked like the leaning tower of Pisa. He had most of his face squeezed up around his ears. Suddenly he felt the magician grab one ear and pull.

'Hi!' yelled Albert, who, despite his fear, had just about reached the end of his tether. He pulled away violently and the magician let go of his ear and dropped something small and cold into his outstretched hand. The audience gasped.

Albert didn't dare to look. The magician grabbed Albert's ear again and dropped another small, cold round thing into his hand. The audience gasped again. He did it three more times, the audience gasped three more times, then the magician laughed and said, 'Albert! Open your eyes!'

Albert opened one eye, which was all he thought he could risk, and looked into his hand.

Then Albert gasped.

'Show your little friends!' said the magician. Albert held up five, shiny fifty-pence pieces and the boys and girls all clapped and cheered.

'Now that is *real* magic!' said the Great Gazebo. 'I thankah yeough! I thankah *yeough*! And I thank you, Albert. Let's all give Albert a big hand!' and the magician giggled and clapped as Albert walked off the stage.

Albert looked down at all his schoolmates, who were clapping and cheering and smiling and laughing. There, in the back row he spotted Fionnuala. She was in a huddle with her friends, talking out of the side of her mouth, telling all her friends how she had never really cared about whether Albert came back or not, and how horrible he was, and then she looked straight at Albert with one of her faces on. As soon as she caught Albert's eye she made a far worse face and stuck out her tongue at him. But Albert just smiled back.

As he was sitting down between the Two

Terrible Ps, Albert heard the magician saying, 'And now I want to introduce you to another friend of mine ...'

He went over to his battered brown suitcase covered with labels from all over the world and took out a ventriloquist's dummy.

'This is Charlie McCarthy,' he said, as he sat the dummy on his knee.

'Aaah!' Albert said to himself as he sat between the Two Terrible Ps.

Both the Ps turned round to Albert and asked, 'What?'

'Oh ... nothing. It doesn't matter ...' said Albert and he began to clap and cheer very loudly.

At the back of the hall, Fionnuala felt a hand on her shoulder.

'*Bwook!*'

She froze and her eyes stood out on stalks. She turned slowly around. It was, surprisingly, The Chicken.

'I was watching you when Albert came off the stage, Feewonuuuuwalla,' said The Chicken. 'See me in my office when the magician has ... *bwook* ... finished ...'

Fionnuala groaned and put her head in her hands, and as she did she heard the laughter of the magician ringing in her ears.

'Eey-hay-hay-hay, eey-hoo-hoo-hoo, UHH-UHH-A-HEY-HOO!'

Other Red Flag Books from O'Brien Press

THE GREAT PIG ESCAPE
Linda Moller

When the farm cat warns Runtling the pig of his approaching fate, this little piggy realises that the trip to market is one which he must avoid at all costs. He warns his twelve pig siblings and together they escape. They find an abandoned farm, but then new owners arrive and the pigs fear that their escape has been in vain. But Nick and Polly Faraway have strange, alternative ideas about farming that might work to the benefit of pigs and humans. Maybe there can be a happy ending after all!

Paperback €6.50/STG£4.99

BOOM CHICKA BOOM
Liz Weir

Stories old and new, with participation rhymes and playful verses, from a noted storyteller. Full of magic and drama, the book consists of the following stories: 'Going to Granny's', 'The Rabbit's Tale', 'Wee Meg Barnileg', 'Master of All Masters', 'Long Bony Finger', 'Boom Chicka Boom', 'The Tailor and the Button', 'Rathlin Fairy Tale' and 'A Riddle Story'.

Paperback €6.95/STG£4.99

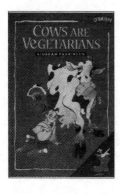

COWS ARE VEGETARIANS

Siobhán Parkinson

Michelle lives in the town. When she visits her country cousins, Sinéad and Dara, she is not impressed by farm life. She finds wild animals in the garden, lambs in the kitchen, muck everywhere and no shops or street lights. How will she ever manage to put with it all? And how on earth will Sinéad and Dara manage to put up with Michelle?

Paperback €6.50/STG£4.99

ANIMALS DON'T HAVE GHOSTS

Siobhán Parkinson

Dara and his sister, Sinéad, are visiting their know-it-all cousin Michelle in the city. They're on a fun tour of dead bodies, sliced-pan ducks, midnight feasts, sticky buns and lots more! But Dara is scared of the stuffed animals in the Natural History Museum and Michelle just can't help teasing him. That's when Dara's not getting lost, becoming a movie star or being airlifted by giant balloons ... One thing is certain, Dublin is never a boring place.

Paperback €6.50/STG£4.99

ADAM'S STARLING
Gillian Perdue

Adam is shy and a dreamer, and when he is picked on at school by Rory and the bullies, Adam doesn't know what to do. His parents are too busy to help, so he must face this problem alone. Then a scruffy little starling follows him to school and seems to be in need of a friend, too. Will Adam find the courage at last to stand up for himself?

Paperback €6.50/STG£4.99

WALTER SPEAZLEBUD
David Donohue

Walter Speazlebud is a whizz at spelling backwards, just like his favourite person: his grandad. Grandad says he has 'the power of **Noitanigami**' (that's 'Imagination' backwards). But Walter's not sure if Grandad is just going a bit funny in the head. Or can 'the power' really make people, and animals, go backwards in time? So when his horrible teacher, Mr Strong, starts picking on Walter, he'd just better watch out. Because when Speazlebud's about, it spells **elbuort** for all bullies ...

Paperback €5.95/STG£4.50

WOLFGRAN
Finbar O'Connor

Granny has sold her house to the three little pigs and moved into the Happy-Ever-After Home for Retired Characters from Fairy Tales. But the Big Bad Wolf is still on her trail! Disguised as a little old lady, the wolf is causing mayhem as he prowls the city streets, swallowing anyone who gets in his way, including several very polite policemen. Hot on his heels are Chief Inspector Plonker, Sergeant Snoop and a very clever little Girl Guide in a red hood. But will they get to the wolf before he gets to Granny?

Paperback €6.50/STG£4.99

WOLFGRAN RETURNS
Finbar O'Connor

Inspector Plonker is once more on the trail of his old enemy, Wolfgran, but this time he's going undercover. Disguised in a pantomime wolf suit, can the Inspector and his faithful sidekick Sergeant Snoop escape being throttled by Granny Riding Hood's nephew, blasted by the Chief of Police, hand-bagged by a bus queue full of very cranky old ladies and run over by the terrifying vets from TV's 'Pet Patrol'? And will they manage to stop the Big Bad Wolf before he gets to the Grand Gala Bingo Night and finally makes a meal of Little Red Riding Hood?

Paperback €6.50/STG£4.99

JULIET'S STORY
William Trevor

Where would you find talking snails,
fighting queens, Welsh witches and
winter sunflowers? In stories, of
course, and that is why Juliet loves
them. On a holiday in France, Juliet
hears lots of stories – from her grand-
mother and from the toymaker who
sells wind-up animals on the quayside.

Juliet wants to be a storyteller too, and when she embarks
on a mission to rescue the little trout in the restaurant fish
tank, she begins an adventure which turns into her very
own story.

Paperback €6.50/STG£4.99

Send for our full-colour catalogue